GRETEL KILLEEN

My Sister's a
Sea Slug

Illustrated by Zeke and Eppie

from Zeke, Eppie and Gretel

MY SISTER'S A SEA SLUG
A RED FOX BOOK 0 09 944807 6

Published in Great Britain by Red Fox,
an imprint of Random House Children's Books

PRINTING HISTORY
First published in Australia by Random House Australia Pty Ltd, 1999
Red Fox edition published, 2003

1 3 5 7 9 10 8 6 4 2

Red Fox books are published by Random House Children's Books,
61–63 Uxbridge Road, London W5 5SA,
a division of The Random House Group Ltd,
in Australia by Random House Australia (Pty) Ltd,
20 Alfred Street, Milsons Point, Sydney, NSW 2061, Australia,
in New Zealand by Random House New Zealand Ltd,
18 Poland Road, Glenfield, Auckland 10, New Zealand,
and in South Africa by Random House (Pty) Ltd,
Endulini, 5A Jubilee Road, Parktown 2193, South Africa

THE RANDOM HOUSE GROUP Limited Reg. No. 954009

A CIP catalogue record for this book is available from the British Library.

Printed and bound in Great Britain by Clays Ltd, St Ives plc

www.kidsatrandomhouse.co.uk

The Random House Group Limited supports The Forest Stewardship
Council® (FSC®), the leading international forest-certification organisation.
Our books carrying the FSC label are printed on FSC®-certified paper.
FSC is the only forest-certification scheme supported by the leading
environmental organisations, including Greenpeace. Our
paper procurement policy can be found at
www.randomhouse.co.uk/environment

A message from your author...

A big 'Gooday' from the other end of the world, otherwise known as Australia. An Aussie life is very different to yours. The sun shines nearly all the time and on Christmas Day even Santa has been known to wear his cozzie. It is an enormous country full of extraordinary creatures that you might never find anywhere else. In this book you'll read about a **snapper fish**, which doesn't snap at all, a **tailor fish**, which can't even sew, a **man-o'-war jellyfish** which can kill with its sting, and a **stone fish** which looks like a harmless stone lying in the sand under the water, but will poison you if you tread on it.

So now put your cozzie on and let's dive into this adventure.

It's not every day that your sister shrinks to the size of a strawberry, gets tangled in your yo-yo and ends up in outer space. And it's not every day that you have to pretend your tennis racquet is your sister while you disguise yourself as a sheep, catch a ride on a rocket, meet the man in the moon, zoom on a space motorbike, get kidnapped by Martian girls and chased by King Neptune all the way to Planet Sock, where you have to rescue your sister who is about to marry a fish! And it's not every day that you have to ride on a meteor and the amazing speed stretches you and your sister long and thin like pieces of spaghetti, so that when you finally do get home, you both get sucked down the bathtub plughole. But that's what had happened so far today.

'Blub this blub is blub all blub your blub fault!' blubbed long, skinny Zeke as he and very long, skinny Eppie whooshed and swooshed down the plughole.

'IS NOT!' blurted Eppie as her head popped up for just a second from under the bubbly water.

On and on they swirled and twirled, through the wide looping plumbing pipes that ran under the bathtub, and under the bathroom basin, and under the shower, and under the you-know-what, which luckily was very clean.

They zooshed and pushed and gooshed
and rooshed round bends and loops,
faster than a waterslide until all of a
sudden Zeke and Eppie smashed into
something round, green and slimy.

Splat kapow! went Zeke as he bounced
into the great big slimy green thing's arms.
Splat wow! went Eppie as she boinged off
the green thing's great big belly, bounced
off its elbow, somersaulted off its shoulder
and landed splat-ping on its head.

And that's where Zeke and Eppie sat,
shaking with fear until Eppie got brave
enough to look down and see just what
the huge green thing was.

'Frog!' Eppie said, shrieking like a car alarm. 'I can't believe it's you!'

'Crebbit Eppieeeeeeeeeeeeeeeeeeee,' croaked the frog excitedly, as he gently removed the long skinny Eppie from the top of his head and gave her a very wide-mouthed frog kiss on the side of her long skinny cheek.

'Oh gross! What is going on?' mumbled Zeke, who was so revolted that both his eyes rolled inward and stared at his nose. 'Why would anyone ever kiss Eppie if they weren't getting paid for it!'

'Oh, I'm sorry,' said the frog politely. 'How rude I seem to be. Let me introduce myself a little more formally. I'm Flop the Frog, you may remember me. You put me in your sister's bed when she was only three.'

'And then I was so scared I scooped him up and flushed him down the toilet,' said Eppie.

'And down the pipes I flowed and rolled until I was found by a beautiful girl who has since become my wife,' said Frog.

Then up swam a glorious goldfish wearing the very same ring on her fin that Mum had lost four years ago while she was doing the washing up.

'Meet Mrs Frog, the fish,' said Flop the Frog.

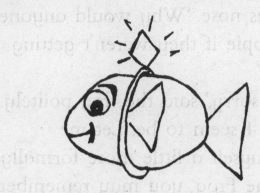

'Flip!' gasped Zeke excitedly, recognising the goldfish.

'Zekie Poops!' squealed Mrs Flip Frog the fish. 'I haven't seen you since you were washing out my bowl and accidentally tipped me down the sink.'

And so in the wide plumbing pipes under the bathroom Zeke and Eppie hugged Flop the Frog and Flip the Fish and met the baby twins, Frish and Fog. Hug hug squish squish on and on it went

10

until finally Flip the Fish said, 'We'd better get you home straight away before your mum discovers you're missing.'

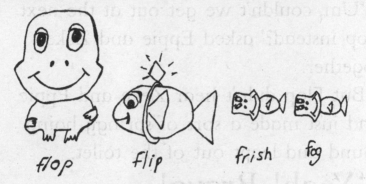

flop   flip   frish   fog

So Flop the Frog said, 'I'll take you back, but you'd better hold on tight!' and with a crebbit-vroom he started swimming back up the pipes with Eppie and Zeke perched on his shoulders like long skinny backpacks.

'Bye, bye, bye,' said Flip, Fog and Frish.

'Goodbyeeeeeeeeeeeee,' said Zeke and Eppie as Flop the Frog swam like a speedboat and carried them swiftly up the pipes until he stopped underneath the bathroom toilet.

'Now,' said Flop the Frog, 'hold on tight because I'm going to jump up and out of the toilet.'

'Um, couldn't we get out at the next stop instead?' asked Eppie and Zeke together.

But Flop didn't hear Zeke and Eppie and just made a sort of springy boing sound and leapt out of the toilet.

'Yeah! Bravo! Cooleroony!'

Except for one thing. Zeke and Eppie slid off Flop while he was in midair and they plopped back into the water. Then Flop landed on the button that makes the toilet flush and whoosh, swoosh, long skinny Eppie and long skinny Zeke were flushed down the plumbing pipes again.

This time they were going so fast they could not be stopped by anything! In seconds they passed Flip and Fog and Frish. Bubble, swoosh, whirl and swirl, down the bendy twisty turns, up and down and round and round through the pipes that ran under their house, and then through the pipes that connected to their neighbours, and their neighbours' neighbours and under their friends' houses, and under Buster the Bully's house, and under the homes of goody-two-shoes Clair Blump and Darryn Pinky. (Oh pong!) Then on they went, and on and on, through bigger pipes that went under the shop that was up the road, under the park, and under the school and under the home of Miss Snailheadface and under the park that was twelve streets away. Faster and faster and faster they went until all of a sudden, with a great big splash, they came to a stop and found themselves in a stormwater drain, which is a huge sort of grubby deep cement box pond, where all the litter and goop gets trapped so it doesn't flow into the rivers and sea.

'Oh yuk! This water's dis-gust-ing!' said long skinny Eppie as she doggy paddled with an old plastic bag on her head.

'Yes,' said Zeke as he tried hard not to touch the oil slicks, bits of vegetables and litter. 'For once in your life you are right. This place is completely revolting, but still not as revolting as you.'

'Is so,' said Eppie.

'Is not,' said Zeke.

'Is so,' said Eppie.

'Is not,' said Zeke.

'Is so.'

'Is not.'

'Is so.'

'Is not.'

'Is so.'

'Is not.'

14

'Is snot?' boomed a thick, grubby voice. 'Did I hear you say snot? Where? Where? Let me see it. I just love to eat snot.' And just then Zeke and Eppie saw the most disgusting grey slippery slimy eel slithering in the filthy water.

'Where are you?' it said. 'I can't see a thing in this murky muck. It's made my eyes so bad. Pleeeeeease, tell me where you are.'

'We're not telling you, you horrible burpbreath,' said Zeke as he tried to climb onto a passing oil drum.

'Never mind telling me where you are,' slurped the eel. 'I'll find you by sniffing you out.

'You can try to escape from here,' he smirked, 'but you never will. This filthy pond is bottomless and its walls are so covered in barnacles and slime that you could never climb out. And if you try to escape by swimming through to the river that's just over there, you'll find a metal net that will stop you. It is a net that divides the polluted stormwater from the clean water that flows fresh on the other side, and you will never get through.'

'Nooooo!' screeched Eppie, kicking and screaming as she felt the whoosh of the eel around her legs.

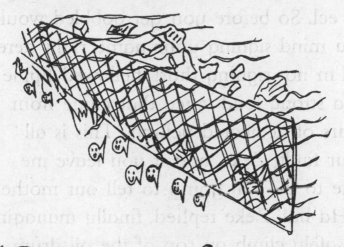

'Get away from me!'

'Ah, excuse me, Eppie,' interrupted Zeke politely. 'I realise you're busy but if I could please have your attention for one moment. I'm just wondering if you would sign the small document that I have written here using an old red texta, that I found in the water, and a wet paper bag. It states that you acknowledge I have helped you to the best of my ability and that you do not hold me in any way responsible for the fact that you are about to be eaten by an eel. So before you get gobbled would you mind signing your name right here.'

'I'm not signing that!' bellowed Eppie in a strong loud voice that came from years of dedicated yelling. 'This is all your fault, Zeke, and if you leave me here to die I'm going to tell our mother.'

'Ha ha!' Zeke replied, finally managing to safely climb on top of the oil drum. 'You can't tell anybody anything if you're eel breakfast. Ha ha ha ha ha ha!'

'Ah, yum!' said the nearly blind eel as he licked his lips. 'I'm getting very hungry now.'

'Help!!!!!!!!!!!!!!' roared Eppie. 'Help me, Zeke!'

'Oh be quiet, Eppie,' Zeke replied calmly as he sat safely on his oil drum. 'You don't honestly think that anything in the entire world would eat something as revolting as you? That eel will take one little lick of you and then probably go and be sick.' And with that Zeke laughed so hard and loud that he lost his balance and fell from the oil drum, back into the disgusting water.

'Help!' cried Zeke. 'Help, Help, Help, Help!!!!!!!!!!!'

'Aha, two of you,' slurped the eel. 'But which one will I eat

'. Mmmmmm I wonder.' The eel did
eenie meenie miney mo to decide just who
to have for main course and who to
have for dessert while Eppie started to
swim away very quietly. Then, when she
was a safe distance from the eel, she kept
herself afloat by paddling with her long
skinny feet and began to blow air into
the plastic bag that had been sitting on
top of her head.

Like a balloon, the plastic bag grew
bigger and bigger as Eppie blew. Bigger
and bigger and bigger until it was just
like a raft. Then, when no more air
would fit, Eppie sealed the plastic bag by
tying a knot in the handles.

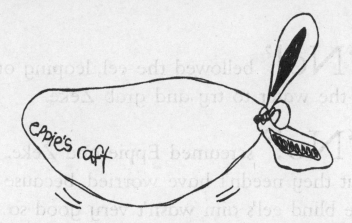

'Hey Zeeeeeeeeeeeke!' Eppie called as she climbed on board her raft. 'For a zillion dollars you can climb on too.'

'But I haven't got a zillion dollars,' Zeke whispered urgently while the eel, who kept forgetting just who was eenie and who was meenie, continued with his *eenie meenie miney mo*.

'Well how much have you got?' said Eppie like a smarty pants.

'I haven't got any money with me,' said Zeke. 'But in my piggy bank at home I've got about two dollars fifty.'

'All right,' said Eppie. 'That'll do. Now quickly climb on board.'

21

'**No!**' bellowed the eel, leaping out of the water to try and grab Zeke.

'**No!**' screamed Eppie and Zeke. But they needn't have worried, because the blind eel's aim wasn't very good so he missed Zeke completely and bit the big plastic bag instead.

eppie's raft

Now, you know how when you're blowing up a balloon and you suddenly let the air out, the balloon sort of shoots speedily around the room while making a raspberry sound? Well, that's exactly what happened to the blown-up plastic bag with Zeke and Eppie on board.

'Ppppppphwwwwt!' it went. 'Zoom, vreeet, blurt, phlup!' Then up rose the plastic bag from the surface of the water, flying like a mad mosquito.

'This might fly us over to the land,' gasped Zeke, holding on as tightly as he could.

'Yes, we're nearly there!' called Eppie excitedly. But she spoke too soon because the plastic bag was quickly running out of air.

'Fizzle phwat blop phew sigh,' went the balloon as the last of the air wheezed out of the plastic bag and Zeke and Eppie crashed back into the big scummy pond.

'Oh no!' wailed Zeke and Eppie as the eel's head with his chomping jaws popped up again nearby.

'Oh yes,' said the eel with saliva dripping from his mouth. 'Now you are both mine!'

'Swim!' hollered Zeke.

'Ah der,' said Eppie. Because she was obviously not going to sit down right there and then and drink a cup of tea and eat a strawberry doughnut.

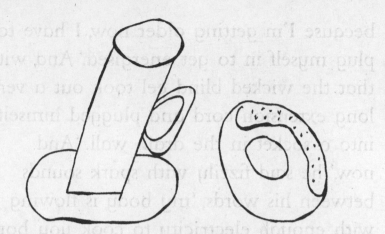

And so they swam as fast as they could
to the wire-mesh fence that separated the
muck from the clean water.

'Hell-o,' said the eel as soon as they
arrived. 'So good of you to come.'

'Oh no! It's you again,' said Zeke,
sounding like a very scared squeaky
mouse. 'But how did you know we'd
swim here to the fence?'

'Because I'm the one who told you
about the fence. Don't you remember?
And I told you about it on purpose,
because this is where my power point is.
You see I'm actually an electric eel but,

because I'm getting older now, I have to plug myself in to get energised.' And with that the wicked blind eel took out a very long extension cord and plugged himself into a socket in the drain wall. 'And now,' he said fizzily with spark sounds between his words, 'my body is flowing with enough electricity to cook you both to a crisp. And there's no way you'll get past me because humans are too big to squeeze through that fence.'

'We're not,' replied Eppie. 'You can't see, so you probably haven't noticed but Zeke and I are very skinny and we can easily swim through the gaps in that fence!'

Then Zeke and Eppie each took a huge breath and dived underneath the thick murky water. They used their hands to find a gap in the fence then they both tried to swim through at exactly the same time and of course got stuck. So they did what any sensible brother and sister would do at a time like this, they started arguing under water (which only the most experienced of fighting brothers and sisters can actually do).

'Blubble blah bla blobble blo,' said Zeke.

'Blahblablha blo bla blop,' replied Eppie.

'Blip blo,' said Zeke.

'Blip blot,' said Eppie.

'Blip blo.'

'Blip blot.'

'Blip blo.'

'Blip blot.'

'Oh that fabulous arguing,' simmered the blind eel. 'Just keep making that noise and I'll swim towards the sound and eat you raw. Or else I could just attach myself to the fence and fry you when you try to swim through again.'

Gulp!!

'LET'S GO!' yelled Zeke.

So they both took a big breath and began to wriggle-swim through the litter-covered fence to the clear blue crystal-clean waters of the river on the other side.

'How dare you!' screeched the eel as he realised his breakfast was escaping. And with that he hurled himself at the fence and sent such an enormous electric zap through the wire that four weird things happened:

1. Eppie's hair frizzled into a bunch of fizzy curls.

2. Zeke and Eppie shrank to the size of a big toe.

3. Zeke and Eppie discovered they could breathe and talk under water, and . . .

4. Zeke's shirt blew off, which left him wearing only school shorts and his Barbie undies.

'Oh well at least we're free,' shrugged Eppie underwater.

'Yes,' moaned Zeke. 'Free to go home, get busted by Mum and spend the rest of our lives in a circus as the freaky midget people.'

'Oh stop whingeing,' said Eppie. 'Do you wish you'd got eaten by an eel instead?'

'No,' said Zeke.

'Well I wish you had,' said Eppie, laughing so much that bubbles of water came out of her ears, her nose, the ends of her toes and of course her belly button. 'Hey, let's have some fun before we go home.'

'OK,' said Zeke, who'd already got bored of sulking. 'Let's check out this cave!' And off they swam happily into the cave.

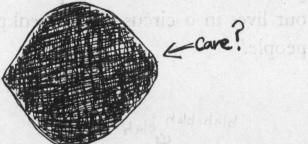

←—Cave?

But it wasn't a cave. It was a wide open mouth. And Zeke and Eppie swam like water babies into a groper's gob.

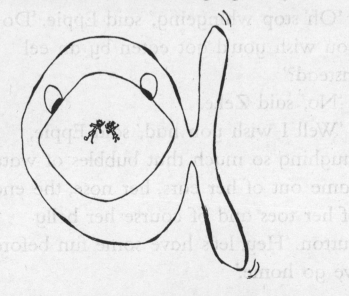

'All right,' said Eppie, as she sat in the dark on the floor of the big fish's stomach. 'I think that even the most stupid thing in the world would say that this situation is all your fault.'

'Well, considering you are the most stupid thing in the world,' said Zeke, 'I guess you'd know.'

'I am not the most stupid thing in the world,' said Eppie.

'No. I'm sorry,' said Zeke. 'You're probably not the most stupid thing in the world because I guess it is possible that a worm's bottom is more stupid than you.'

'Aaaaaaaagh,' roared Eppie, as she hurled herself at Zeke. 'That's it! I've had enough of you.'

'Well, I've had enough of you,' said Zeke, struggling to defend himself as Eppie dived on him. 'My life was ruined the minute you came along. And that was before I turned three.'

'Well,' said tiny Eppie with her teeny weeny hands on her teeny weeny hips, 'imagine how I felt when I was a baby and came home from the hospital with my mum and realised a pig lived in our house.'

'I am not a pig!' said Zeke as he tried to get Eppie into the sort of hold that you see on 'World Championship Wrestling'.

'Oink oink oink oink,' said Eppie.

And so they wrestled in the fish's stomach with Eppie pretending to be world famous wrestler *Eppie the Exterminator* and Zeke trying hard to think of a name other than *Zeke the Zebra*. Eppie was a fabulous wrestler but finally Zeke got her in a crumbling crush hold and Eppie burst into tears.

'What's the matter, ding-dong face?' said Zeke softly, trying to be as nice as could be so he didn't get into trouble.

'Are you hurt? I didn't hurt you, we were just pretending, you started it, it's not my fault, it's all your fault, I'm telling Mum and she's going to be furious especially if you don't stop crying.'

'I sob can't sob stop sob crying,' sobbed Eppie.

'Why?' said Zeke. 'Are you a leaking tap?'

'Aaaaaagh,' thundered Eppie angrily. 'I can't stop crying because, in case you haven't noticed, we're stuck in a fish's stomach.'

'Oh yeah,' gulped Zeke, trying not to cry.

'I want to go home,' whimpered Eppie. 'It's dark in here and sort of sticky, and worst of all it stinks. We also have no idea where we're going or where we will end up. This fish could be heading for

Antarctica or the Amazon or the lost underwater city of Atlantis. We might never get out of here or maybe it will take years and years, 'cause we'll have to wait until this fish dies and vultures start to pick at its flesh and make a hole for us to climb out!'

'Don't worry,' said Zeke, thinking about giving Eppie a cuddle but not wanting to catch her girl's germs. 'I promise we'll get home.' And then he started to climb the fish's stomach wall. Up and up and up he went in the dark, like a world famous rock climber, until he reached the very top, where he found nothing.

←nothing

So he climbed back down the other
side to Eppie.

'There's no way out,' said Zeke.

'Don't be dumb,' said Eppie desperately,
'there has to be.' And so she began to
climb. Up and up and up she went until
she got to the very top, where she

found **nothing** and began to
climb back down again.

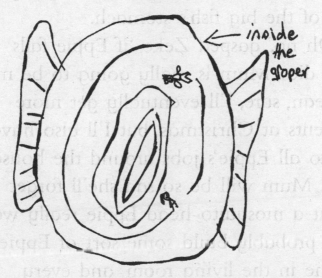

inside
the
groper

'Be careful,' said Zeke.
'What?' called Eppie.

'I said **be careful!**' yelled Zeke a little louder.

'What?' Eppie yelled back. 'I can't hear you!'

'I said **be careful,**' bellowed Zeke as loudly as he possibly could.

'All right, there's no need to yell!' roared Eppie, letting go of the wall to cover her ears. And with that she fell down, down, down from the very high top of the big fish's stomach.

'Oh no,' gasped Zeke, 'if Eppie falls and dies, Mum is really going to be mad. I mean, sure, I'll eventually get more presents at Christmas, but I'll also have to do all Eppie's jobs around the house. And Mum will be so sad she'll forget what a mosquito-head Eppie really was and probably build some sort of Eppie shrine in the living room, and every night we'll all have to stand around it and sing songs like the one Eppie made up last week called "Boys, boys, boys we love you, come and give us a kiss".'

'Oh Eppie, don't die!' Zeke called suddenly as his sister continued to fall. 'I don't really think you're completely stupid, Eppie. I think you're brilliant . . . and you just hide it very well.' And then he ran to the corner where he thought she might land with his arms out ready to catch her. But no sooner had he arrived in the corner than Eppie seemed to change her direction and be about to fall in a completely different place.

'I'll save you, Eppie!' Zeke called. But then Eppie seemed to swerve a bit and be about to land somewhere else. So round and round Zeke ran. From here to there from there to here, holding his breath and preparing himself for the thump of Eppie's weight. But he needn't have worried because when Eppie landed he didn't feel a thing . . . because she landed BLUMP on the ground beside him.

'Oh no, this is the end of both of us,' murmered Zeke as he took a deep breath and ran to his sister's side. But before Zeke could even kneel down beside her, Eppie did the most amazing thing and bounced back up to the top of the stomach again.

'Whooppeeeeeee,' she yelped as she boinged back down and then bounced up and up once more. 'This stomach wall thing is like a trampoline,' said Eppie.

'You have a go.' And so Zeke did.
With a big breath and a jump he
bounced up and down with Eppie.
Boing off the stomach sides,
boing off the top,
boing bong kapow
in every direction until they both
stopped giggling for a moment and
happened to hear a strange sort of
rumbling sound.

'Did you hear that?' asked Eppie in
midair.

'Not really,' said Zeke. 'Let's keep
bouncing.'

And then there was another rumble.

'Did you hear that?' said Eppie more
urgently.

'Yeah,' said Zeke. 'It sounded like
Grandpa when he's just finished dinner.'

And then there was another rumble,
bigger and louder and longer this time.

'Hold on!' screamed Eppie, as she tried to stop bouncing. 'I think there's going to be an explosion!'

And sure enough that big fish did a, how shall we say, bottom burp, ah . . . fart . . . and Eppie and Zeke flew straight out that fish's bottom. (Sorry, but that's what happened.)

'Hooray,' said Zeke. 'We're free at last!'

'But . . . where are we?' said Eppie.

There were no clues, there were no signs. There was only water all around. And they weren't in the cool calm river any more but deep, deep underneath the sea surrounded by rocks and seaweed and old shipwrecks and the sound of Celine Dion singing the theme song from the movie *Titanic*.

'Oh this is scary,' said Eppie softly.

'I know,' said Zeke, 'I can't stand this song either.'

'No, I'm talking about what's behind you!' whispered Eppie. 'Don't move, but it's a shark.'

'Excuse me, Eppie,' Zeke replied, 'but if you don't mind me saying, when you put the word *shark* in a sentence you don't also use the phrase *don't move*. You use,

quick move as fast as you can. Which is exactly

what I plan to do.'

But it was too late. Because as fast as a small person wearing nothing but Barbie doll underpants and school shorts might be able to swim, it is absolutely nowhere near as fast as a shark wearing no clothes at all.

Quick as a wicked wink, the shark zoomed up behind Zeke and opened his big shark jaws.

Zeke and Eppie's hearts pounded like jungle drums. 'Do something,' said Zeke.

'You do something,' said Eppie. And with that they both did something together. They both fainted from fear.

'Hehehehehe,' giggled a school of irritating middle-size devil fish. 'Those two tiny things are going to be eaten. Let's go closer so we can watch!'

So the devil fish swam in closer to get a better look and giggle even louder, 'Hehehehehehehehehehehehehehehe hehehehehehehehehehehehehehehehehe

hehehehehehehehehehehehehehehehehe
hehehehehehehehehehehehe.'

'Oh shut up,' said the shark and
with one big gulp it swallowed the entire
school. Then he gently nudged Zeke and
Eppie with his nose and said, 'Hey wake
up. There's no need to be scared. I'm not
going to eat little tadpoles like you. You
wouldn't begin to fill me up and would
just get stuck between my teeth.'

Slowly Eppie and Zeke opened their
eyes, but they took one look at the
shark's razor-sharp teeth and immediately
fainted again.

'Oh dear,' groaned the shark. 'No one ever believes how sweet and gentle I am. I have exactly the same problem trying to get a girlfriend. What I need is a disguise so I don't look so scary.'

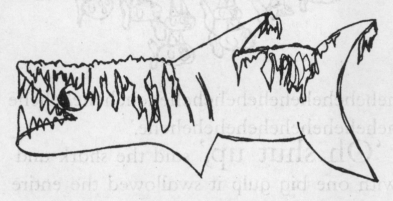

And with that he covered himself in seaweed, gently scooped Zeke and Eppie up on to his dorsal fin and used his nose to 'knock knock knock' on the nearest clam shell.

'Yes, what is it?' said a very snoozy clam who had obviously been woken up by the knocking.

'Hello,' said the shark in a high girly voice that sounded a bit like Posh Spice.

'I was wondering if you have a phone I could borrow.'

'No,' replied the clam rudely. 'There's a public phone you can use on the corner.'

'Well, would you look after these two small animals in your shell while I just go and make a call?' asked the shark sweetly.

'Oh sure,' said the clam sarcastically. 'I'll put them in the guest room, shall I? Don't be ridiculous, I'm a clam in a shell, there's hardly enough room for me!' And the rude clam slammed her lid shut.

'Sssssssssoooooooo, what have we here?' hissed a slippery sea snake. 'Two sssssssssssssssssmall animalssssssssss needing a babyssssssssssitter. I'm sssssssssimply perfect for the job.'

'But can I trust you?' asked the shark nervously.

'Of courssssssssssssssssssssssssse you can,' said the snake. 'I'm jusssssssst like you deep down inssssssside, a really, really sssssssssssssssssuper guy.'

So the shark felt safe and went off to find a phone.

'No, I would never eat anything as small as these little things,' continued the snake after the shark had left, 'but I'd use them as bait to catch something bigger!' And so, while the good, kind shark went to ring his mum and ask for advice, the snake prepared to stick Zeke and Eppie on a fish hook.

'Excuse me!' said Eppie suddenly

waking up. 'But if you seriously think you're going to put that hook through our gizzards, you've got a big surprise on the way.' And with that she head-butted the snake so hard in the nose that he immediately began to see sparkling stars and hum *Ring a ring a roses* so loudly that the water policeman arrived.

'Hello, hello, hello, what's all this kerfuffle?' said Sergeant Stingray.

So Zeke and Eppie tried to explain about the eel and the shark and the clam and how they needed to get back on land with humans.

'Humans!' gasped the stingray. 'But I haven't a clue what to do with a human. Um, um, um . . . I know, I'll take you to the mermaid castle to visit the royal family. Mermaids are a bit like humans. And if they're not home, I'll try the penguins, because at least they walk a bit like you.'

So Zeke and Eppie rode to the mercastle on the stingray's back, just like it was a magic carpet.

'Yoo-hoo,' called Sergeant Stingray as he tapped on the enormous doors of the fortress wall that protected the mercastle. 'Yoo-hoo, police here. Is anybody home?'

'Well hello, Sergeant,' purred Catriona the catfish who was snoozing on the fortress wall.

'Why hello, Catriona,' said Sergeant Stingray. 'I wonder if you could let me into the castle.'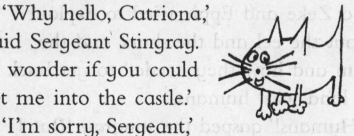

'I'm sorry, Sergeant,' Catriona meowed. 'But you see the castle is preparing for an attack from our enemies and I can't let anybody in.'

'Not even if I gently scratched behind your ears?' teased Sergeant Stingray.

'Well, let's try and see,' growled Catriona softly.

And so the stingray used his very long pointy sting to gently scratch behind the ears of Catriona the catfish, and she loved it so much and purred so loudly that all the neighbours started to yell, 'BE QUIET! WHAT'S THE RUCKUS?' and 'STOP IT OR I'LL HOSE YOU!' (which is more than a little odd considering they were underwater).

'Oh that was purrrrrrrfect,' said Catriona. 'And now you may bring the little things in. Is it true they're friends with Shark!'

'Shark!' gasped Zeke and Eppie, and promptly fainted again.

The enormous gates rolled open and the stingray swam up the golden pathway to the coral castle door carrying Zeke and Eppie.

'Da da da da,' blasted the trumpet shells when Sergeant Stingray arrived. 'Two tiny humans here to see the royal family,' said the sergeant. Then he placed the unconscious Zeke and Eppie on the lovely moss rug in the huge reception hall and swam back to continue scratching Catriona.

'Oh my, what have we here?' said the queen mermaid, who wasn't very big herself but had long green hair and a shiny golden body. 'How can we look after these little things just when we're preparing to fight for our lives and protect our castle from an enemy who wants to kill the royal family, move into our wonderful castle and make all the subjects of the kingdom their slaves? Oh boohoo, it's really all too much.'

'What is it, my dear snuggle-bum-head?' called the king as he continued to put on his shell armour. 'Shouldn't you be preparing to escape with the children in the royal carriage? I know the sea horses are prancing and ready.'

'Oh Kingy poops,' replied the queen. 'The problem is that these two small humans have arrived on our doorstep and I . . .'

'I'll look after them!' called the king and queen's daughter, Milly the mermaid, as she came sliding down the banister on her long silvery tail. Then she scooped up the unconscious Zeke and Eppie and tucked them into her Barbie shoulder bag.

'All right then, let's go to the carriage, quick sticks,' said the king. 'We must abandon the castle and leave immediately before the enemy attacks.'

'We can't, Dad,' said Milly. 'My brother, Max the merboy, isn't here.'

merking merqueen merprince merprincess

'Well, what on earth is he doing?' said the queen.

'I think he's playing footy in his bedroom,' Milly replied.

'Oh, how a merboy plays football I'll never know,' said the queen. 'And if I've asked him once I've asked him a thousand times, not to do it in his bedroom. Max! Max! If you don't get down here right this instant you'll have no fun for a week.'

'Was that Mum yelling?' said Zeke waking up, because the queen sounded just like their mother.

'Are we home?' asked Eppie excitedly.

'Oh no,' said Zeke looking round. 'I don't think we're home. I have a sneaking suspicion my worst fear has come true and we're trapped in a Barbie bag.'

'What makes you think that?' asked Eppie breathlessly.

'Well, because there's a big pink plastic jeep, some miniskirts, high boots, hair brushes and a ridiculously big bosomed blonde doll all squished in here beside us.'

'Yippeeeeeeeeeeeeeeeeeeeeeeeeeeeeeeeeeee eeeeeeeeeeeeee!' squealed Eppie.

'Did you hear that?' said the queen. 'I think that was the war cry of the enemy approaching!'

'Quick, my Queenie,' said the king. 'Take Milly up to Max and hide them both in his bedroom.'

Up the long pebbled staircase they went, through the sparkling hallways glittering with lost pirate treasure and then into Max's bedroom, which surprisingly looked just like Zeke's, with walls covered in posters of wrestlers, basketball heroes and surfers.

'Cool,' Zeke gasped as he peeked out of the bag.

'Yo Mamma,' said Max as the queen entered his bedroom.

'Would you please stop playing football in here!' said the queen. 'And get under the bed with your sister.'

'Oh gross,' said Max. 'Do I have to? Can't she hide under the bed in her room?'

'No she can't,' said the queen. 'She is your sister and I'm your mother and I'm telling you to get under the bed and look after Milly until the battle is over. Now be good. I'm going down to help your father load the cannon fish into the cannon.'

And so, under the bed went Max and Milly and the Barbie bag while the maids put all sorts of fabulous food on top of the bed; ice-cream and hot dogs and crisps and fizzy drinks and milkshakes and lollies and the most enormous cake with a sign that clearly said THIS FOOD IS ONLY TO BE EATEN IN AN EMERGENCY!

'I'm bored,' said Max angrily.

'Me too,' said Zeke from inside the Barbie bag.

'Hey! Who said that?' asked Max as he looked suspiciously at the Barbie bag. Then slowly he took a look inside and what he saw gave him such a fright that his eyes rolled upwards and he went completely still and very, very cold, and he sort of **froze.**

'Quick, pinch him, Milly,' said Eppie. 'That's what I'd do to Zeke.'

'Good idea,' said Milly. 'How many times?'

'Eighteen dillion,' said Eppie.

'Don't be stupid,' said Zeke. 'If you pinch him, he'll only pinch you back. That's what I'd do if Eppie pinched me at a time like this. And besides, there must be a better way to unfreeze him.'

'I know! Let's sit on him,' said Milly.

'Why?' said Eppie and Zeke.

'Because there's nothing he could do to stop us,' laughed Milly. 'But I suppose we

don't really have to make him come
back to life. I mean, it's pretty good
having him frozen stiff 'cause he's much
kinder and nicer this way.'

'Gosh girls are geeks,' said Zeke.

'Are not,' said the girls.

'Are so,' said Zeke.

'Are not.'

'Are so.'

'Are not.'

'Are so.'

And so the argument continued . . .

Blah! Blah! Blah! with the
three of them yelling and shouting over
each other and getting very hot. So hot
in fact that the air under the bed started
to get very warm and Max began to get
really hot and sort of begin to melt.

'Be quiet!' said Milly urgently. 'Max is
starting to move again and I'd begun to
hope that he'd stay stiff so that when the

enemy came to attack we could use him as a shield.'

'I heard that, Milly,' said Max. 'And before you use me as a shield I'm going to use you as ammunition in my slingshot and fire you at the enemy. And when you land in the middle of their army and start blabbing away like usual, you know what our enemies are going to do? Offer to surrender and give us all their precious things if we do just one simple thing, and that is make you shut up!'

'Ha ha!' laughed Zeke. 'That's what they'd do with Eppie too.'

'Who are you?' asked Max.

'I'm Zeke,' said Zeke. 'Pleased to meet you.'

And so the merboy and the tiny human boy became best friends because the shared dislike of sisters can be very bonding for blokes.

'Want to play basketball?' asked Max.

'You can be the little ball and I'll throw you through the hoop.'

'OK,' laughed Zeke.

So they crawled out from under the bed and played basketball like pros, throwing Zeke again and again through the hoop above the door. And the girls? Well, they had a fabulous time dressing tiny Eppie up in all Barbie's outfits (the cowgirl, the business executive, the nurse, the firefighter, the rollerblader, and the nun), all of which were a little big. But luckily, one costume fitted perfectly, the fabulous Barbie bikini.

'You look beautiful,' said Milly.

'No you don't. You look gross,' interrupted Max very rudely, which was probably a sign that he was starting to fall in love with Eppie.

'Hey, watch out!' Zeke yelled to Max. 'Keep your eye on me!' But it was too late. Zeke came crashing down and landed in the cake that was on top of the bed and splattered cream and goop all over the girls. So the girls picked up some cake and threw it back at the boys. And then the food fight was on. Squishy fruit and sloppy cake and gluggy milkshakes all went flying across the room. Splat, splat, splat, splat in the face, in the hair, in the eyes, and Zeke and Eppie and Max and Milly were laughing and laughing and laughing and laughing, which is absolutely fantastic, except for one important thing, they were supposed to be hiding quietly under the bed so the enemy didn't know they existed.

Bang! went the enemy on the door.

'Oooops,' went Zeke, Eppie, Milly and Max.

Bang! Bang! Bang!

went the enemy on the door again. But this time the brothers and sisters stayed silent.

'Shouldn't we say something?' said Eppie.

'Like what, egghead? Sorry, there's no one here?' said Zeke.

'Well, it's very rude just to ignore them.'

'All right,' said Zeke. 'You go and meet the enemy at the door and the rest of us will escape out the window while you get eaten.'

'We could throw the rest of the food at them,' Milly said.

'No one's ever been killed by a cake,' said Max.

'They could have been if our mum had cooked it,' mumbled Zeke and Eppie.

'Open this door immediately!' said a voice that was so scary even the walls of the mercastle began to shake with fear.

Zeke and Eppie and Max and Milly needed an idea, quick smart. What on earth were they going to do?

'We could dig a tunnel through the floor,' said Max.

'Um, we could see if the enemy is ticklish?' said Zeke.

'Or Zeke could just breathe on them,' said Eppie. 'Because his stinking breath would definitely knock them out.'

'OK we're coming in,' said the enemy. 'Prepare to be captured.'

'Oh, has anyone got any lipstick?' asked Eppie.

'BE QUIET,' said Max. 'They're coming here to kill you, not ask you on a date.'

'Quick, hide under Max's surfboard,' said Milly. And so Max and Milly and Zeke and Eppie dived onto the floor and held the cuttlefish surfboard over their heads. Then they waited for the enemy to break down the door and turn them all into slaves.

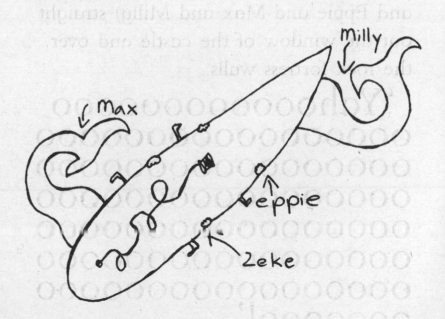

'You know, there might only be one soldier out there and he just happens to have a big booming voice,' said Milly hopefully as the four new friends lay huddled and hiding underneath the surfboard. But oh boy was she wrong, because just then the door was smashed down by such a tremendous force of soldiers that they caused a sort of tidal wave that shot the surfboard (and Zeke and Eppie and Max and Milly) straight out the window of the castle and over the rock fortress walls.

'Yahooooooooooooo oooooooooooooooooooo oooooooooooooooooooo oooooooooooooooooooo oooooooooooooooooooo oooooooooooooooooooo oooooooooooooooooooo ooooooo!'

Over the kingdom the surfers rode, first hanging underneath the board, then sitting on top of it, then kneeling, then standing, then handstanding. They were cool, they were hot, they were really funky dudes. They thought they had definitely escaped from the enemy until the wave ran out of power and the underwater surfboard dragged to a stop.

'We can't stop, we're not safe yet!' said Max to Zeke, Milly and Eppie. 'Can't you hear that thump, thump, thump?

That's the enemy soldier crabs following us!'

And so they paddled, with Zeke and Eppie using their tiny hands and the merchildren using their tails. Paddle, paddle, splash, splash they went past undersea forests and rivers and farms until they finally came to a town where they hoped they could find help and shelter. But not a living creature could be seen.

'Helloooooooooooooo,' called Eppie as they paddled through the spooky town.

'Hellooooooooooooooooo, Eppie,' laughed Zeke until Max gave him a wedgy.

'Is anybody there?' called Milly hopefully, but no one answered. All the shops and homes were sealed up tight, not even an oyster, or anemone was open. Shells lay empty and abandoned because every living thing had left the city to escape from the enemy.

'This place is a ghost town,' said Eppie in a squeaky mouse voice.

'That's right,' snapped an echoing, ghoulish voice. 'A ghost town is exactly what it is.'

'Aaaaaaaaaaaaaaaaaa
aaaaaaaaaaaaaaaaaaaaaaaaa
aaaaaaaaaaaaaaaaaaaaaaaaaa
aaaaaaaaaaaaaaaaaaaaaaaaaa
aaaaaaaaaaaaaaaaaaaaaaaaaaa
aaaaaaaaaaaaaaaaaaaaaaaaaaaa
aaaaaaaaaaaaaaaaaaaaaaaaaaaaaa
aaaaaaaaaaaaaaaaaaaaaaaaaaaaaaaaa
aaaaaaaaaaaaaaaaaaaaaaaaaaaaaaaaaaaaa
aaaaaaaaaaaaaaaaaaaaaaaaaaaaaaaaaaaaaaaaaaaaaaaaa
aaaaaaaaaaaaaaaaaaaaaaaaaaaaaaaaaaaaaaaaaaaaaaaaaaaaaaaaaaaaaaaaaaaaaaaaaa
aaaaaaaaaaaaaaaaaaaaaaaaaaaaaaaaaaaaaaaaaaaaaaaaagh,' screamed Zeke and Eppie and Max and Milly.

'Oh be quiet,' snapped the ghost snapper fish. 'You've already woken the dead.'

'How dare you speak to us like that?' roared Milly furiously. 'If you don't help us I'll have your head chopped off and your guts taken out and have you fried up for our dinner.'

'Ha ha,' laughed the snapper. 'You're too late, because that's already happened to me. And you'll find no one here to help you because they've all escaped to Happy Hill.' And then he swam away leaving Max and Milly and Zeke and Eppie all alone, like the vegetables you leave on your plate.

'Don't worry, I'll get us out of here,' said Zeke. Then he reached out to hold Milly's hand but he grabbed a ghost octopus tentacle instead.

'Hi, loverboy,' said the octopus. 'How about a cuddle?'

'Aaaaaaaaaaaaaaaaaaaaaaaaaaaaaaaaa aaaaaaaaaaaaaaaaaaaaaaaaaaaaaaaaaaa aaaaaaaaaaaaaaaagh,' squealed Zeke, just like an old lady who's discovered mice living in her undies. He tried to push the octopus away, but Zeke's two hands didn't stand a chance against the eight tentacles of the octopus and soon he was being cuddled and kissed all over the place.

'Let go of him,' ordered Milly, who was actually a little bit jealous.

'No way,' said the octopus. 'This hunky boy is mine. So say goodbye because we are off to Happy Hill to find a priest and get married.' Then she whirred her tentacles like the propellers of an outboard motor and took off with Zeke.

'Grab on to the octopus, you guys,' yelled Eppie, 'and we'll get a free ride out of here.'

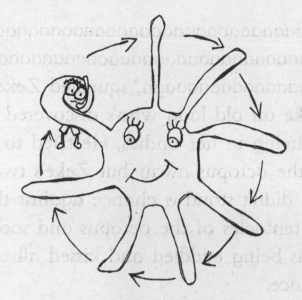

So Eppie and Max and Milly each grabbed on to part of the octopus and hitched a ride to Happy Hill. Well, almost. You see after two or so hours the octopus got so exhausted she suddenly stopped and fell asleep. Well, of course Max, Milly and Eppie tried to wake the octopus by pretending to be alarm clocks ringing in her left ear. But at the same time Zeke was successfully trying to keep her asleep by singing lullabies in her right ear.

'Stop trying to keep her asleep, Zeke,' said Eppie, making a face that was so scary it would make a rat curl up and die. 'Can't you hear the thump, thump, thump of the enemy's marching soldiers? We have to get out of here as fast as we can.'

But the octopus was fast asleep and not even a squeeze on the bum from a passing prawn could wake her up. So Zeke and Eppie and Max and Milly sat on the sea bed like bits of old chewing gum until an unemployed fairy godfish just happened to swim by.

'Hello,' said the lovely fairy godfish with long golden hair. 'Do you need help? I desperately hope so. I have to do at least one good deed a day and what with every living thing having moved to Happy Hill it seems like I haven't had a thing to do for ages. Oh please tell me that you're in urgent need of help. Oh please, please, please, please, please.'

'We *are* in urgent need of help. We need to get to Happy Hill,' said Eppie and Zeke and Max and Milly as the clomp-clomp-clomp of clomping feet clompered closer.

'Good!' said the fairy godfish. 'Make a wish please and it will be my command.'

Well now, I don't know if you've ever been asked to make just one wish but it's a pretty hard thing to do. So imagine how hard it would be to make one wish if there were four of you? Everyone wanted something different: Zeke wanted a BMX bike, Milly wanted her favourite dolls to come to life, Eppie wanted Christmas every day and Max wanted a fighter jet. The fairy godfish listened to one wish, then the next, then the next and the next and started to get quite dizzy. Until finally she collapsed on the sea bed and giddily said, 'Perhaps you should just wish to get to where you're going.' And with that she waved her magic wand, and said, 'Biddly bill off to Happy Hill,' and Zeke and Eppie and Milly and Max were immediately zapped to Happy Hill.

Once they arrived all the creatures of Merkingdom who'd been hiding on Happy Hill came out and hugged and kissed and sort of squishy-cuddled Max and Milly. At times it was a little slimy, but what can you do when your royal subjects want to worship you? You can hardly say, 'Go away you are too squishy.'

'Hooray!!!!!' the royal subjects bubbled and blurted as they clapped their fins.

'The royal family is safe! Hooray! Hooray!' There was joy and lots of laughter and the whole crowd joined in the chorus when Eppie sang her new favourite song, 'My Brother's in Love With an Octopus'. But then one shy little darting pink and green striped curious fish interrupted the excitement by asking, 'But where are the king and the queen?'

'Aren't they here?' asked Max.

'Oh no!' sighed Milly.

'Don't worry, we'll find out where they are,' said Zeke and Eppie at exactly the same time and so then they had to say 'jinx' as well.

But the enemy had destroyed all the undersea telephones and captured the courier crabs and pigeon fish. How could they possibly find out where the king and queen were? The only way to send a message to anyone seemed to be by smoke signal, but you can't do that underwater. So the four adventurers had a meeting to think of anything they could do to find the king and queen. They dragged every possible idea from their brains and then fell asleep exhausted under green moss blankets. They were very sad and scared and lonely . . . but not as lonely as when Zeke and Eppie woke up.

'Where are Max and Milly?' gasped Eppie.

'I don't know,' said Zeke. 'But I think I've gone blind, because I can't see a thing!'

'You can't see because you've got a long note sticky-taped to your forehead and hanging down over your face,' groaned Eppie as she pulled the note off.

'Ouch!' said Zeke. And Eppie began to read out loud.

Kidnap Note

Ha ha! We have kidnapped
the merprince and princess
and it was so simple. We
just told those royal
merchildren that we could
take them to their parents.
And they believed us! Ha ha
and so now we are taking
them to our undersea-bed
hideout to keep them as
slaves in our kitchen while
we go off to capture the
Mercastle and become rulers
of Merkingdom. Lots of love,
two brown smelly sea
slugs.

'Well, that's interesting,' said Zeke.
'No it's not, it's terrible,' whimpered
Eppie.

'What's interesting, Eppie, is the fact that those sea slugs are so conceited they had to show off in their letter. You look. They not only told us who they are, but where they're going and what they're planning to do. You know, I wouldn't be at all surprised if they haven't bothered to hide their trail.'

Sure enough, two long silver sea slug lines glowed on the sandy undersea floor showing exactly where the kidnappers had gone.

'This is great,' said Eppie. 'All we have to do is dress up as sea slugs, follow the silver trails and rescue Max and Milly from the hideout.'

'Dress up as a sea slug! I can't do that!' said Zeke. 'It's all right for you, Eppie, you already look like one.'

'Ha ha ha,' muttered Eppie, like she'd just heard the worst joke in the world. 'Actually, I planned for us to go to the tailor fish and see if they could sew us each a costume.'

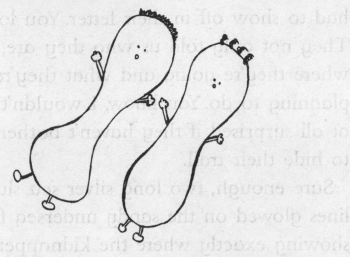

Two hours later, after a visit to the tailor fish, Zeke and Eppie both looked exactly like sea slugs. 'OK,' said Eppie, 'let's follow that trail.' So they wriggled along for about a metre (which is a very long way when you're tiny and dressed in a sea slug costume) and then they wriggled another metre, and then the silver path stopped.

'Oh fabulous,' said Zeke grumpily. 'Now where do we go?'

'I think we go down that rather large hole there,' said Eppie. And so they wriggled down the hole in the sand.

It was dark and spooky for most of the twisting turning tunnel that led to the hideout, and the scurrying of soldiers' feet echoed against the walls. 'Where are all the soldiers going?' wondered Zeke and Eppie. But they needn't have wasted even a second thinking about it because just then they came to a door on the side of the tunnel. And when they opened the door, which was guarded by two mussels, they saw the most enormous room filled to the brim with the entire enemy army.

The soldiers were armed with swordfish and were listening to their General as he bellowed, 'Within this underground room is every one of my soldiers. Congratulations on all that you have done. We have the merprince and merprincess and tonight we will finish defeating the soldiers at the mercastle. The king and queen have not yet been found, but of course they are hiding within their castle. So tonight, when we capture the castle and make it ours, we will also capture the king and queen. We will put them in a blue-bottle-tentacle jail from which they can never escape. And I shall be the ruler of the sea!'

The soldiers let out an almighty battle roar and sang the first verse of 'For He's a Jolly Good Fellow'. Then they marched like a machine to the weapons room to prepare for the final battle that night.

Zeke and Eppie snuck away to continue down the tunnel searching for Max and Milly. The tunnel grew wider and before long they came to a doorway that led to a large living room. And in the centre of that room, sitting in a huge conch shell were Max and Milly being guarded by two fat man-o'-war jellyfish.

'Huuuuuh!' gasped Milly when she saw Zeke and Eppie.

'Ssssssssshhhhhhhhhhhhhh, or they'll get caught,' said Max. 'We have to sit here patiently and wait and see just how they're going to rescue us. They might stab the guards, or trap them in a net, or tie them up with man-o'-war-eating seaweed, or spray them with superglue so they set really hard.'

'Oh, that's a good idea,' Zeke said after overhearing Max. 'You don't happen to have any superglue do you, Eppie?'

'No, of course I don't. But I do have something that just might catch the attention of the man-o'-war guards. I have my new dance that I made up last Saturday and I'm sure these guards would love it. What about if I do the dance over in the corner and you untie Max and Milly while the guards are watching me?'

Before Zeke had a chance to take a breath and say, 'Gee Eppie, that is without a doubt the dumbest thing you've ever said,' Eppie had slithered right up to the guards and already started her dance. Up in the air her little arms and legs flew, spinning and pirouetting and doing the twist, moon-walking like Michael Jackson and then doing her own form of breakdancing.

Well! The guards just couldn't believe that a small human dressed as a slug had managed to enter the hideout. And they could not believe that the small human was dancing. And they really absolutely could not believe how incredibly dreadful her dance was! The men-o'-war watched

in complete shock and then both died of
embarrassment.

So Max and Milly and Zeke and Eppie
ran back through the tunnel and popped
back out the hole. Then
they sealed all the
soldiers inside
forever by
asking a stone
fish to sit on
the entrance.
When word
of the enemy's capture spread over
Happy Hill, the creatures organised a
great colourful marching parade all the
way back to the mercastle. There were
cheering crowds and seaweed streamers
and four huge proud prancing seahorses
carrying Zeke, Eppie, Max and Milly.

When the parade arrived at the castle
all the happy creatures were greeted by
the king and queen, who had escaped

from the enemy by hiding in the huge pile of washing and wet towels that lay on the floor in Max and Milly's bathroom. Everybody cried and cheered of course, and then Zeke and Eppie were escorted upstairs where the Barbie bag was found and Eppie was dressed by the servants in one of Barbie's long princess dresses, and Zeke was dressed in one of Ken's suits. The clothes were a bit big, but Zeke and Eppie still looked like Brad Pitt and Jennifer Aniston.

Then it was downstairs to the magnificent ballroom and an unbelievable feast of desserts like rainbow jelly (fish). A band was playing a little off-key because the trumpet fish didn't have a tuna, but no one minded and everyone danced, even Eppie, though only the brave guests dared to watch her. Every creature of Merkingdom celebrated the greatest party of their lifetime. And then, when the laughter and happiness were loudest, the king rose from his glorious golden shell throne to make an official announcement.

'Silence!' he ordered and everyone hushed. 'The time has come to honour those who have saved us. Zeke and Eppie, please come forward.'

Zeke and Eppie went up onto the stage, looking beautiful, handsome and brave.

'We of Merkingdom thank you from the bottom of our hearts for rescuing our young prince and princess and for trapping the enemy,' said the king royally. 'And, in return, Marlin the Magician will grant you any wish you desire.'

'Well?' asked Marlin the Magician. 'What will it be?'

'Oh, we'd like to go home,' said Zeke and Eppie excitedly.

'Easy,' said the magician. 'Just tell me where you live.'

So Zeke and Eppie gave their land address and the magician said, 'Land! Oh that's a bit difficult. Yes, well . . . How can I say this? Basically, I could return you to somewhere within Merkingdom, turn you into toads, or wake you from a timeless sleep.'

'Oh,' said Eppie with a disappointed sigh. 'Well, could you possibly put a spell on our mother so that when we get home she forgets we've ever been away?'

'Yes, I can certainly give that a go,' replied the magician. 'And if you get home and your mother isn't a toad then you'll know the spell has worked.' With the wave of a wand the spell was cast and it was time for Zeke and Eppie to leave the party and try to find their way home.

'Wait, wait, wait,' said the queen. 'I have organised two wonderful dolphins to give you both a lift.'

Then the kingdom bade farewell to Zeke and Eppie and promised to stay in touch. 'Come and visit us some time,' said Eppie to Max and Milly. 'You can get to our place by swimming along the river, through the stormwater drain, along the pipes and up the toilet.' And then they left on the dolphins' backs.

'Wahoooooooooo!' shrieked Eppie and Zeke as the dolphins jumped and dived and played with them underneath the sea. 'You know,' said the dolphins as they swam, 'we can only take you as far as the beach, because we're saltwater dolphins and we can't swim up rivers.'

'Oh yes,' said Zeke happily. 'That's OK. You drop us off on the beach and we'll get home from there.'

So the dolphins swam and swam, then gently dropped the children on the golden sandy beach, giggled goodbye and went off to play.

'I'm just going for a quick walk to try and work out how far it is to our home,' said Zeke. But within seconds he was back looking like he'd just seen Godzilla.

'What's the matter?' asked Eppie.

'We're nowhere near home,' he mumbled in shock. 'We're stranded on a desert island!'

And that's when they wrote **HELP** in the sand, and climbed up the only palm tree on the island to see what they could see.

NOTHING!

'We could put a message in a bottle,' said Eppie.

'We haven't got a bottle,' said Zeke.

'Well,' said Eppie, seriously starting to think they were probably going to die on the island but trying very hard to be cheerful, 'we'll just have to look out for passing ships and in the meantime let's go for a swim. It is completely stinking hot here and it's making me tired and if we fall asleep then we'll never spot the ships.'

So Zeke and Eppie dived into the clear blue sea but even the water couldn't wash away their tears. So they got out and lay their sopping wet, sad little bodies on the sand and promptly fell asleep.

So then what?

Well, now I don't know if you know what happens with the sun and the sea and the way the world works but the sun lifts water droplets from the seas and the rivers and draws them up towards the sky where the droplets all form clouds, which then form the rain that waters all the earth. It's called evaporation and, strangely enough, that's what the sun did with sopping wet little Eppie and sopping wet little Zeke. It thought they were tiny water droplets and lifted them up to join the clouds.

It was cold up on the cloud and the change of temperature woke Zeke and Eppie.

'Oh well, at least we're off the island,' said Eppie, holding on as tight as she could while she peered over the edge of the cloud.

'Yeah,' said Zeke sounding glum. 'And we could spit on bullies' heads from up here and they'd never know it was us.'

'Hey, no need for that,' said a passing homing pigeon. 'Perhaps I can help you.'

'Do you know where our home is?' asked Zeke and Eppie.

'Well no, but tell me your names and I'll find some bird who does.' And with that he took out his mobile phone and called back to bird base.

'Chirp chirp squawk screech,' gaggled the homing pigeon into the phone and then hung up. 'Problem solved,' he said to Zeke and Eppie. 'The stork who delivered

you when you were born is on his way.
He knows where you live so you'll be all
right now.' And then the homing pigeon
flew away.

Now Zeke and Eppie felt a lot happier
and began to bounce around on the
cloud like they did on their mum's bed.
Then the stork arrived, ticked Zeke and
Eppie's names off on a roll and mumbled
something about paperwork. Then he
loaded them into the bag around his
neck and flew and flew and flew
and flew, flap flapping very loudly.

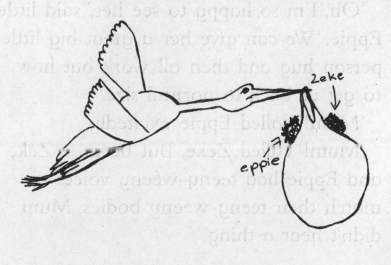

Zeke

eppie

'There's your home down there,' squawked the stork.

'Yippeeeeeeeeee!' squealed Zeke and Eppie.

'I wonder if Mum will be happy to see us?' said Eppie. 'Although, considering she's been put under a spell she might not even know we were gone.'

'I don't know,' said Zeke, 'but we're about to find out. Because there she is in the garden putting clothes out on the line.' And sure enough, in the afternoon light they saw their mum.

'Oh, I'm so happy to see her,' said little Eppie. 'We can give her a great big little person hug and then all work out how to get us back to normal size.'

'Mum!' called Eppie excitedly.

'Mum!' called Zeke. But because Zeke and Eppie had teeny-weeny voices to match their teeny-weeny bodies, Mum didn't hear a thing.

'Mu-u-um!' called Eppie.

'Mu-u-um!' called Zeke. But still Mum didn't hear a thing.

So, once the stork was flying right over their garden, Eppie and Zeke decided to jump out of the stork's bag and down to earth and really surprise their mum.

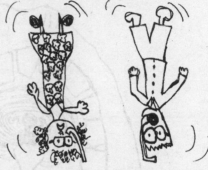

'Thank you, Stork,' they both said politely as they jumped and began to float downward.

'Mum . . . Mum . . . Mum . . .' Zeke and Eppie called as they drifted closer. But still their mum didn't hear a thing. So louder and louder and louder they called, '**Mu-u-um, Mu-u-um.**'

Then finally their mum looked up to see two small things flying through the sky, coming closer and closer and closer.

And, as she gazed in surprise, Mum's mouth fell wide open and Zeke and Eppie fell inside.

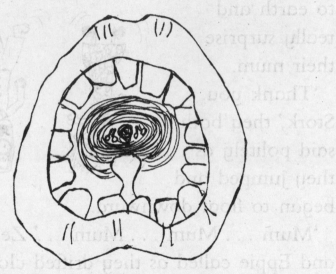

'Gulp,' said Zeke and Eppie's mum. 'I think I just swallowed two flies!'